Marie-Danielle Croteau

Fred's Midnight Prowler

Illustrated by Bruno St-Aubin
Translated by Sarah Cummins

First Novel

Formac Publishing Company Limited
Halifax, Nova Scotia

Formac Publishing Company Limited acknowledges the support
of the Cultural Affairs Section, Nova Scotia Department of
Tourism and Culture. We acknowledge the financial support of
the Government of Canada through the Book Publishing Industry
Development Program (BPIDP) for our publishing activities.
We acknowledge the support of the Canada Council for the Arts
for our publishing program.

Canadian Cataloguing in Publication Data
Croteau-Fleury, Marie Danielle, 1953-
[Mon chat est un oiseau de nuit. English]
Fred's midnight prowler
      (First novel series)
      Translation of: Mon chat est un oiseau de nuit.
      ISBN 0-88780-522-1 (pbk)
      ISBN 0-88780-523-X (bound)
I. Saint-Aubin, Bruno. II. Title. III. Series.

PS8555.R6185M6313 2000   jC843'.54   C00-950158-4
PZ23.C768Fr 2000

Formac Publishing
Company Limited
5502 Atlantic Street
Halifax, NS B3H 1G4

Distributed in the U.S. by
Orca Book Publishers
P.O. Box 468 Custer, WA
U.S.A. 98240-0468

Distributed in the U.K. by
Roundabout Books (a division
of Roundhouse Publishing Ltd.)
31 Oakdale Glen, Harrogate,
Printed and bound in Canada   N. Yorkshire, HG1 2JY

Table of Contents

To the real-life Jessie and Miguel, from whom I borrowed freely to create the characters in the book. And to the staff and students at Ann Hébert School, who were at the heart of my long stopover in Vancouver.

1
Supergran

From behind we must look like a forest in autumn. Miguel, who is Bolivian, has black hair. Jessie is Belgian and he has red hair. And then there's me, the Canadian, with hair as yellow as the tiles in my grandmother Jackie's kitchen

We were sitting side by side on the steps and discussing a problem I was worried about. For nearly a week my cat, Rick, had been spending his nights outside. He would come back home only to sleep. He hardly ate a thing.

He didn't want to play
anymore.

I wasn't at my own house. I
was spending the summer
with Jackie in Vancouver. I
love my gran but without my
cat, I was feeling like only
half a person. There was no
Fred-Rick anymore. I was just

plain Fred. It was like I'd shrunk.

I had told Jackie that morning how worried I was. So she called Miguel and Jessie to come and help me. They live in the same neighbourhood and we had quickly become friends.

"We should start an investigation," suggested Jessie.

He loves mysteries, and here was a fine one.

"Or you could send Rick back to your parents' house," suggested Miguel.

No way. I had to work like a dog to get my cat. I wasn't about to send him away.

"May I join you?" asked Jackie, bringing a snack.

She sat down with us on the steps. One more tree in the forest. This was a grey tree, with a topknot.

"I think Jessie's right," she said. "We should start an investigation."

Then, pushing her tiny round glasses back up on her tiny nose, she added, "Maybe your cat has found a girlfriend, Fred. If so, you wouldn't want to spoil his fun, would you?"

"You think Rick might be in love with a Vancouver cat?"

"Why not? My mechanic's dog fell in love with a German shepherd!"

Grandmother Jackie paused to take a bite of cookie.

"If Miguel and Jessie sleep over, you can start tonight by

putting a tail on your cat. What do you think?"

"Rick already has a tail," Jessie objected. English is his second language. Jackie explained that she meant we could follow Rick when he went out.

"My mother doesn't want that I go out at night," said Miguel. He was just learning English. He had a very musical way of speaking.

"Don't worry," Gran reassured him. "I'll call her."

"You can tell her that you are our leader," said Jessie.

He was the opposite of Miguel. Miguel was calm, but Jessie was excitable. Miguel was stocky, while Jessie was built like a rake.

"True," I said. "We do need a leader."

"A litre of what?" asked Miguel.

We all laughed, and explained the difference between leader and litre. We three boys were in agreement. In her Supergran outfit, Jackie would be the perfect leader for our team.

She had worn the outfit the evening before, when her bridge partners came over. The other three old ladies cracked up when they saw her.

The outfit consisted of purple leggings, pink roller-blades with gold sequins, and an imitation Ninja Turtle helmet, all topped off with a filmy little cape in shiny neon green. She looked like the atomic ant in cartoons.

Jackie thought she was too old to go tearing around after a cat on her in-line skates.

"Don't worry," Miguel tried to persuade her. "In that outfit, no one will recognize you."

"Oh, all right," she said finally. "Since you insist."

She stood up and shook the cookie crumbs out of her skirt.

"I will be your quart—I mean your leader."

2
A dead-end street

At eleven o'clock, Rick decided to go out. Finally! We three boys were drowsing off on the coach, in our skates and helmets. Fortunately, Jackie was keeping watch.

We sprang into action. We didn't want to wake the neighbourhood, so we bumped down the steps on our bums. Then we clomped across the street, Jackie herding us along like a crossing guard.

By the time we reached the bike path, Rick had disappeared

from sight. We looked right, we looked left, but there was no sign of him. We had no idea which way to go.

Jackie decided for us.

"We'll explore in this direction," she said, pointing to the right. "If we don't find anything, we'll try the other way tomorrow night."

We set off in silence. It took all our breath just to keep up with Gran. At this time of the night, there was no one else on the track and she raced ahead. She wasn't going that fast, but she set a steady pace. It was exhausting.

We skated for about twenty minutes without seeing a thing. Then suddenly, a black shadow darted out from the side of the track and slipped between us to the other side.

No doubt about it. That was a cat. But we couldn't tell whether it was Rick. It had come and gone like a flash of lightning, like a breath of wind.

We decided to follow it anyway. Chasing after a shadow was better than chasing after nothing at all. Even if it was the wrong cat, perhaps this cat would lead us to Rick.

For half an hour, we zigzagged through the streets on the tail of the phantom cat. Sometimes an overturned garbage can gave us a clue, sometimes a sharp miaow from the darkness.

Then we came to the end of a dead-end street, and there were no more clues.

There was a little grey house, as silent and slumbering as the others—maybe more so. Hunched over on itself, it looked as if the sun must never reach inside.

"It looks like a haunted house," whispered Jessie. "I bet a witch lives there. Maybe that was the witch's cat we were following. That would explain why it disappeared so suddenly. It probably went right through the wall!"

"Come now!" Gran interrupted. "You're going to give yourselves nightmares. Let's head back home."

None of us liked that place

and we were glad to leave. But since we were all thirsty, we decided to have a drink first. Gran turned around so we could take the water bottles out of her backpack.

At that very instant, a mournful squeak pierced the night. We looked toward the house. The side door was slowly closing as a black-and-white shadow slipped inside.

3
Call the firefighters!

That night I slept badly. I was haunted by horrible images. Rick, soaking wet, struggling to jump out of a witch's cauldron. My poor little kitten, tied up, tortured, cut into pieces. In my dream I cried out and my scream woke me up.

It was seven in the morning. I looked through the house for Rick, silently, to keep from waking the others. Rick was not there. Usually he came home around eight o'clock.

I decided to wait for him outside. I crossed Beach Avenue and took the walk along English Bay. It was a beautiful morning. As each sunbeam hit the water, it made a little golden star.

I wished I could take a little beach spade and shovel

the stars into my heart, to fill up the black hole that had grown there during the night. But I couldn't capture the stars, so I just kept on calling Rick. There was no response.

At eight o'clock I returned to the house.

Jessie and Miguel were still asleep. Gran was bustling around the kitchen. I sat down on a stool and told her about my nightmares. She gave me a big hug.

"After Miguel and Jessie wake up and we have breakfast, we'll go back there," she promised. "You'll see, there's nothing to be worried about. There are no witches and Rick is certainly not being held prisoner.

Honestly! What a story!"

At nine o'clock, my two friends were still snoring and I was beginning to panic. Rick hadn't come back. I was certain that he was in grave danger. We had to do something! But Jackie refused to disturb my friends.

"They need their rest," she insisted. "Let them sleep as long as they want, and they'll be in great shape when they wake up."

So when she wasn't looking, I dropped a pot full of spoons on the floor. That roused them.

"Get up! Hurry!" I begged them. "Rick is in danger."

Emergency or no emergency, Miguel took the time to eat

two bowls of cereals. With sliced bananas on top!

"Calm down, Fred," he kept saying. "Good detectives have to keep their cool."

In my opinion, this wasn't a problem for detectives. This was a rescue job for fire-fighters! Since nobody seemed to understand, I put on my skates and went out and skated up and down on the porch.

Ke-tlunk, ke-tlunk, ke-tlunk! My skates made an unbearable racket on the wooden floor. Jackie and company could not hold out for long. In a few minutes, they had put on their helmets, gloves, and skates, and were ready to set off.

"All right, let's go," sighed Jackie. She sounded discouraged.

This time we weren't so speedy. We were too tired. It was hot and the path was crowded with vacationers.

Tourists strolled along, licking ice-cream cones. They gazed out at the ocean and took pictures. But we had other fish to fry.

At last we reached the dark lane where the little grey house stood. It was just as sunless as I had imagined the night before. At high noon, the place was as sinister as it had been at midnight.

"Well, what now?" asked Gran, turning to me. "What are you going to do?"

It's crazy, but I had not really considered this question. Should I knock on the door and demand my cat, as simple as that? Or should I pretend to be a lost kid and ask to use the telephone, so I could case the joint?

"If you want my opinion," said Jessie, "we should first just watch the house. We have to find a good place to hide."

"It should be far enough away to be safe," added Gran, "but close enough to see what's going on here."

"We can use this," suggested Miguel, proudly proffering his miniature binoculars.

They were in a case he wore around his waist, underneath his T-shirt. No one had noticed them before.

"Well, our problem is solved!" announced Jackie,

smiling her special-occasion smile, which looks like a banana. "Take off your skates, put on your shoes, and follow me!"

Ten minutes later, we were at the apartment of a friend of hers, three blocks away. From the tenth-floor balcony we had an unbeatable view of the dark lane.

"Look!" cried Miguel, after a quarter of an hour.

Mrs. Chisholm, Gran's friend, had just served us enormous bowls of ice cream with chocolate syrup.

Miguel handed me his binoculars.

"Your cat is flying," he said.

What did he mean? Maybe

he got it wrong, and meant to say "Your cat is crying."

I practically tore the binoculars from his hands. I focussed them on the place where Miguel was pointing.

Someone was carrying Rick across the yard towards a little shed behind the house. The mysterious figure went inside and stayed there a minute, then came out again, without my cat.

4
Mamma mia!

I had to do something. I
didn't wait for Gran or
Miguel or Jessie. I just left.
The elevator was at another
floor, so I took the stairs. Ten
flights is a long way down!
All that turning made me
dizzy. I was totally discom-
bobulated by the time I got to
the bottom.

I went off in the wrong
direction.

I ran for about fifteen
minutes before I realized I
was lost. I hadn't recognized
any landmarks, but I didn't

expect to. Last night, we had just followed Jackie and we were worried about witches. We weren't trying to memorize the way!

When I saw a police station, I realized I was lost. I was pretty certain we hadn't gone past it the night before. We would surely have started telling scary stories about cops!

So I was good and lost. I didn't really know how to explain my predicament.

I sat down on the curb and wondered what to do. People going in and out of the police station ruffled my hair and said hi to me.

I kept my eyes glued to my watch, wondering how long it

would take for a miracle to happen. I just said hi back and the people went on their way. No one stopped to help me.

Twelve minutes and fifty-nine seconds later, a pair of black and white shoes approached. They reminded me of Rick. My heart ached. He was a prisoner and I was lost. What a mix-up!

"Mamma mia!" a voice said. "Aren't you Jackie's grandson? What are you doing here?"

I looked up.

"Alfonso!"

It was my grandmother's mechanic! He's the one who keeps her rollerblades tuned up. I had met him two or three times already since I had come to Vancouver.

I told him my sad story. Alfonso's car radio had been stolen and he had come to the

police station to report the theft. But first, he said, he'd take me back.

Since I was lost, I couldn't tell him where to go. So we went back to our starting point, Gran's place, and took the same route all the way to the corner of the little lane.

Alfonso left me there and headed back to the police station. I walked towards the grey house. I was sure I would find my grandmother and my friends hiding in a ditch or behind a tree.

To my surprise, they weren't there. Probably they had stayed to finish their ice cream at Mrs. Chisholm's. Too bad. I couldn't wait for them. I had to take action right away!

I ran to the door and banged on it with my fist. I didn't care about witches or nightmares, I just wanted my cat back! No matter what!

I banged and banged like a madman. Finally someone came and opened the door. What a shock!

5
My brain turned to mush

Behind the half-open door, a girl stood staring at me in silence. She had curly brown hair down to her waist. She wore a flowered red dress. It was wrinkled and worn, but as pretty as she was.

She had hazel eyes with very long, very black eyelashes that accentuated her bright gaze. She was not the witch I had imagined—not at all! I felt I had met a fairy princess instead.

My heart thudded in my chest like the drums at a

circus, before the tightrope walker steps out. I felt like a tightrope walker myself, on a narrow wire, way up high. If I opened my mouth, I might fall.

Anger had brought me to this door. Now I felt as soft and squishy as a marshmallow in the sun. I had to get hold of myself. Probably a spell had been cast on me, and on Rick too. I made an immense effort.

"What have you done to my cat?" I managed to get out. "Where is he?"

"What cat is that?" the girl asked.

She had a strange accent. Her voice was soft and musical, like Miguel's.

"The black-and-white cat

that you shut up in the shed!"

"I didn't shut up any cat. Go and see for yourself, if you don't believe me. The door isn't locked."

I should have run to the shed, but my feet were glued to the doorstep. I couldn't understand what was happening to me. I must have been brainwashed. I was about to do something totally illogical, or nothing at all.

It was so bad I nearly turned and walked away, red-faced, hanging my head, like a puppy that has been scolded. Or had its tail stepped on— *yip! yip! yip!*

Fortunately, Gran arrived just then.

"Fred!" she cried. "What

happened to you? I left right after you did, but when I got here, you were nowhere to be found! I've been looking for you all through the neighbourhood."

Then she turned to the girl and held out her hand.

"Hello, my name is Jackie."

"How do you do? My name is Smaranda," the girl replied.

Smaranda! It sounded like the name of a precious jewel. The girl shook Jackie's hand and smiled. Then she turned to me and held out her hand. When I took it, everything inside me seemed to heat up. Time to call the firemen again!

And call the speech therapist while you're at it. I know what they do because there's one at our school. Right then I seemed unable to speak. My grandmother introduced me to Smaranda.

"We are looking for my grandson's cat," she explained. "Have you seen it, by any chance? A little black-and-white cat. We did see one in the neighbourhood."

"There is a black-and-white cat here," said Smaranda. "But I don't know if it's yours. It's in the henhouse."

I felt my face redden again.

"You told me that you didn't shut up any cat!" I sputtered.

"And I didn't shut up this one. It is free to come and go."

"May we see it?" asked Gran.

"It's busy right now."

"I see. What is it doing?"

"It's sitting on my hen's eggs."

An ordinary grandmother would probably have burst out laughing. But not my grandmother. She takes kids very seriously. Especially (as she told me later) when they tell her the most incredible things.

"I'll show you, if you like," offered Smaranda.

Gran was willing to go along, but I hesitated a moment. Smaranda was as pretty as a dream, but what if we woke up and found it was a nightmare? Maybe she was planning to lure us into the henhouse and lock us up there.

I tried to break out of the spell the girl had cast over me.

"We have to go now, Gran," I said. "We have an appointment!"

I took a step backwards and bumped into Jessie and Miguel. They had eaten every drop of their ice cream before coming to help. It's a good thing I didn't wait for them!

"An appointment?" asked Jessie, surprised. "We don't have an appointment."

I wished I could turn him into a block of cement.

"Don't worry, Fred," said Gran, rescuing me. "I cancelled the appointment. You stay here with your friends. I'm just going to see

if the cat in the henhouse is your cat. Okay?"

And she gave me a wink, which I didn't quite know how to interpret. Did she understand my hesitation or was she making fun of me? Just to be on the safe side, I decided that she was asking us to keep a watch out for her safety.

You can never be too careful!

6
Smaranda and
the three soldiers

We watched Jackie until she disappeared into the henhouse with Smaranda. Then I gave the signal. My two friends and I tiptoed to the window on the side.

Miguel and I knelt down so Jessie, the lightest one, could stand on our backs. We asked him to tell us what he saw, but we got no report. Instead he just stood there on our backs, saying the same thing over and over.

"Well, how do you like that!"

Miguel and I looked at one
another. How did we like
that? Of common accord, we

moved aside and let Jessie fall. As my dad is fond of saying, there's a limit to letting yourself be stepped on!

A second later, I was climbing up onto Miguel's and Jessie's backs. Jessie hadn't told us anything. He just whispered mysteriously, "You'll see."

I pressed my nose against the window. And I saw what Jessie had seen. Rick was sitting on a nest. Smaranda was sitting on Jackie's knee and stroking Rick's head. The three of them looked like they'd known one another forever!

"Well, how do you like that!" I couldn't help saying.

I regretted those words as soon as they were out of my mouth. Miguel, who was fed up with not seeing anything, moved aside and I tumbled down into a pile of straw. My hair was full of it.

"You look like a crow-scare!" said Miguel. "You'll frighten all the birds."

The tension of the last few days seemed to fall then, just as I had fallen into the straw. I began to laugh uproariously, and Miguel and Jessie joined in.

We made so much noise that Smaranda came out. We jumped to our feet, like three soldiers standing to attention: one black-haired, one blond, one redhead.

Smaranda put a finger to her lips and motioned us to come in. Softly we went in, so as not to disturb Rick, who was busy. He was warming the eggs in a hen's nest!

These eggs were extremely valuable. The hen that had laid them was one of a very rare and coveted species. In her old country, Smaranda's mother used to take the birds to market and have them dance.

Smaranda's mother was a Gypsy. When trouble broke out in Rumania, she had fled the country with her daughter, a few clothes, a rooster and four hens.

Two hens had died of seasickness in the freighter that had brought them over.

The third had died a few months after their arrival. The fourth hen was the last fragile link Smaranda and her mother had to the old country.

That's why this hen had been so precious to them. They had called it Tezaur, which means "treasure" in Rumanian. As for the rooster, it was doing fine as cock of the walk. It was vain and noisy and fortunately as tough as old boots.

Tezaur seemed to be adjusting well to her new life. But then suddenly, unexplainably, she died. Then Smaranda's mother fell ill. It was as if the last reminder of the old country had been snatched away.

All this had happened ten days ago, shortly after Tezaur had laid her clutch of eggs. That was when Rick had started to hang out around the neighbourhood.

"He came to help me," said Smaranda, stroking Rick's head. "Thanks to him, we will be able to save the heritage of eight generations of Gypsy

hen dancers. And my mother will get better."

She stopped talking, but nobody moved. We just stared at her, that's all. We gazed at her with admiration.

It was easy to figure out what had happened to Rick. He had been bewitched by a little Gypsy girl, just like the three of us.

Or the four of us, I should say. My grandmother had been the first to succumb to Smaranda's charm. She couldn't tear herself away from that dusty henhouse either.

But it was time to go home. Miguel's mother and Jessie's would be coming to pick them up soon.

"I'm sorry I have to go," I said, blushing. I would have liked to stay with my cat. I missed him!

7
A picnic

The next morning I left the house very early. In less than twenty minutes I was standing in front of Smaranda's house. I had beaten my own speed record, but not Jessie's.

He was already there, pulling off his helmet.

Miguel was not far behind, He arrived a few minutes later, carrying his breakfast in a paper bag.

"I thought I would have a picnic in the woods," he said.

He meant the three cedars standing next to the henhouse.

"What are you doing here?" asked a voice behind us.

In unison, we did an about-face. It was Smaranda. She had come out to throw some vegetable peelings onto the compost heap. The three of us leapt forward to carry the bucket for her.

She laughed at us, but we went with her anyway. The whole day long we kept her company, while she kept Rick company.

My cat nobly continued to keep Tezaur's eggs warm. He had two more weeks to go. I missed him a lot, but at least I wasn't worried about him anymore.

And I was so proud of him! It was because of him that

Miguel, Jessie, and I had met Smaranda. So a lot of the credit came to me! That gave me a lead on the others.

I took that lead whenever I could in the next few days. I was the first to go into the henhouse. I sat down next to Rick and very near Smaranda. Sometimes I even got to her house before they did.

One fine morning, I was the one who discovered my cat surrounded by six tiny chicks. Rick had such a funny look on his face! He looked surprised but happy, and a bit overwhelmed. I think he might have been smiling.

I was as excited as my dad was on the day my little brother Paul was born. I ran

to tell Smaranda, who was just waking up. Then I put on my skates and went back home at top speed.

Gran was just as thrilled as I was. Since my cat was the adoptive mother of these chicks, that meant that Jackie and I were related to them too. It was something to celebrate!

So we packed a picnic basket and went back to Smaranda's. We picked up Jessie and Miguel on the way.

We had an unforgettable picnic. We laughed at Jessie's funny faces and my scary stories about witches. And the funny way Miguel talked!

Smaranda was worried that his feelings might be hurt.

But he was having as good a time as any of us.

"Don't worry, Smaranda," he said, "My feelings aren't heard!"

It was a wonderful day. Smaranda's mother came out to join in the celebrations. She sang a Gypsy song and did a dance. She even had us dancing.

That evening, I was so wiped out! I was asleep before my head touched the pillow. In the middle of the

night, I woke up. I felt a weight on my feet.

I opened one eye. For the first time in two and a half weeks, Rick was sleeping on my bed.

Three more new novels in the *First Novel Series!*

Life without Mooch
by Gilles Gauthier
Illustrated by Pierre-André Derome
Carl's having trouble finding time to write his memoir of Mooch, his favourite dog, because his neighbour Gary is always dropping in with his tiresome little dog, Dumpling. Gary's dad is also spending a lot of time at the house, with Carl's mother. When Carl reads her the first chapter of the Mooch biography Carl gets his first clue that she's beginning to forget some things. She doesn't think that the story is quite accurate. Now Carl's found a strange sock in the living room and he wonders if she's also forgetting about his dad, who died even longer ago than Mooch.

Maddie Wants New Clothes
by Louise Leblanc
Illustrated by Marie-Louise Gay
Maddie hasn't a thing to wear. All her clothes are either too small, or too antique. She's reduced to wearing a ridiculous outfit

that makes her a laughing-stock. Her friend Clementine comes to the rescue. She devises a plan that'll force Maddie's parents to buy new clothes. And Maddie figures out how to get skinny so that she can once again fit into her favourite clothes. Meanwhile, her wonderful Gran is also going through some changes, ones that Maddie doesn't like. Still, only Gran can give Maddie good advice.

Marilou's Long Nose
by Raymond Plante
Illustrated by Marie-Claude Favreau
Marilou can't stop telling stories and white lies. She finds they just pop out without thinking. Now her friends have challenged each other — the first person to tell a lie has to wear a false nose. When she loses the challenge, Marilou wonders if silence isn't better than a lie when it comes to explaining the nose to her father and to her schoolmates. But Marilou's not the only one who tells a story or two. Freddy Busker has a story that everyone wants to believe, and only Marilou can sniff out a lie.

Meet all the great kids in the First Novel series!